GEORGE SHRINKS

GEORGE SHRINKS

STORY AND PICTURES BY WILLIAM JOYCE

HarperCollins*Publishers*

George Shrinks

Copyright © 1985 by William Joyce

First published by Harper & Row, Publishers, Inc., 1985

Printed in Singapore. All rights reserved.

1 2 3 4 5 6 7 8 9 10

First Miniature Edition, 1991

Library of Congress Cataloging-in-Publication Data

Joyce, William.

George shrinks / story and pictures by William Joyce. — 1st
miniature ed.

p.   cm.

Summary: Taking care of a cat and a baby brother turns into a
series of comic adventures when George wakes up to find himself
shrunk to the size of a mouse.

ISBN 0-06-023299-4

[1. Size—Fiction.] I. Title.

PZ7.J857Ge 1991   90-46285

[E]—dc20   CIP

                                                                AC

One day, while his mother and father were out,
George dreamt he was small,
and when he woke up he found it was true.

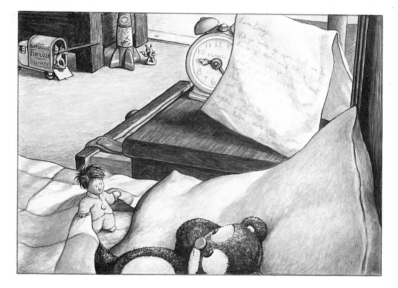

His parents had left him a note:

"Dear George," it said. "When you wake up,

please make your bed,

brush your teeth,

and take a bath.

Then clean up your room

and go get your little brother.

Eat a good breakfast,

and don't forget to wash the dishes, dear.

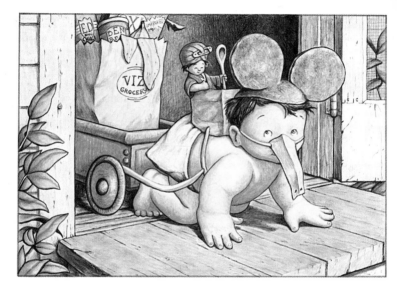

Take out the garbage,

and play quietly.

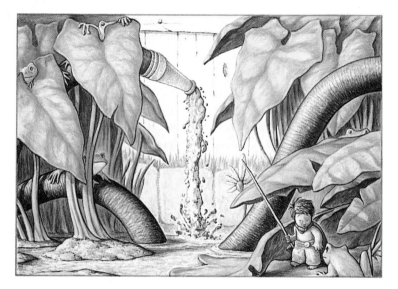

Make sure you water the plants

and feed the fish.

Then check the mail

and get some fresh air.

Try to stay out of trouble,

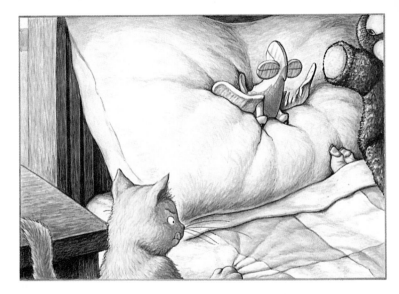

and we'll be home soon.

Love, Mom and Dad."